This book belongs to

The Day I Had a BULLDOZER

Ashley Wall

Vaughan Duck

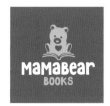

MaMaBear BOOKS

Dedication

To Davis – Embrace your imagination, dream big,
and always believe in yourself!

Text copyright © 2023 by Ashley Wall
Illustration copyright © 2023 by MamaBear Books LLC
Published by MamaBear Books
Visit us on the web – https://www.mamabearbooks.com/

ISBN Hardback: 978-1-960616-00-5
ISBN Paperback: 978-1-960616-01-2
ISBN eBook: 978-1-960616-02-9

Library of Congress Control Number: 2023933892

Hi friends,
Remember real construction vehicles
are for trained professionals only.

Printed in China

Illustrations and design by Vaughan Duck
https://www.vaughanduck.com

I was eating breakfast when my dog, Bobo, started to bark. **A LOT!**

"What is it, boy?" I asked.

"No Way!"

I couldn't believe my eyes.

A bulldozer.

A REAL-LIFE
BULLDOZER!

I raced outside.

What was a bulldozer doing at my house?

As I got closer, I saw my name was on the bulldozer.

"What? This is awesome!"

I knew there was only one thing to do.

Bobo and I hopped in and drove to Noah's house.

As I pulled up, I slammed on the brakes.

Noah was driving a

DUMP TRUCK!

"Check it out, Luke," he called.
"Did you know that dump trucks
can hold about 28,000 pounds?"

"That is a lot of dirt," I said. "Let's test it out."

We had just finished making the most

GIGANTIC dirt hill EVER,

when Bobo leaped past us
and flew right into the center.

He spun in circles,
wagged his tail,

and dug a hole so deep
he disappeared.

Then he poked his head out
like he had heard
something.

Then we heard it, too.

"Whatever is making that noise must be

HUMONGOUS,"

I said to Noah.

We raced to the front yard.

It was Mikey, rolling up in a

STEAMROLLER!

He was sitting up so high
that he didn't see the trashcans.

"Mikey!" I shouted.
"Now the trash cans are flatter than
the pancakes I had for breakfast!"

"Oops! I'm sorry," Mikey said.

"I'm still getting used to driving this thing."

"Whoa, Mikey, let's go to the park before you flatten my house," Noah said.

We cruised to the park. "Look!" I shouted.

Emma was driving an

EXCAVATOR!

This was officially the **best day ever!**

"Hey guys! I was just about to dig a path to the new ice cream shop.

Wanna help?" Emma asked.

"You bet!" We all shouted.

I cleared the path.

Emma filled the dump truck.

Noah made huge piles of rubble, and Mikey...

Wait, where was Mikey?

"No, not the swings!"

I called out as Mikey smooshed the swings flatter than a piece of paper.

"Oops!"

"It's okay, you just have to keep practicing," I told him.

"Mikey,
come flatten a road for us.
I'm getting hungry for a
strawberry ice cream cone
with sprinkles,"

Emma said.

Follow me!

Mikey led the way,
headed straight for the ice cream shop.

"Thank you for clearing
a road to my shop,"
Mr. Popsicle told us.

"You're welcome!
We are happy to help,"
replied Emma.

"Oh no,"
I exclaimed.

I didn't realize how late it was getting.

I had to get home for dinner, because even though I was having fun with my friends,

I still needed to be home on time.

Good thing we made this new road—
I'll be home super-fast!

That night, I told my family
all about my bulldozer adventure.

"Wow, what a day you've had, Luke!"
My dad said.

"I wonder what tomorrow will bring…"

More Stories from

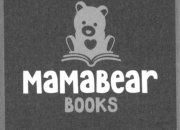

MAMABEAR BOOKS

Detective Stan the Crayon Man
and the Missing Birthday Cake

Colorful County is a vibrant and cheerful place where crayons live, but today something is afoot! Pretty Pink baked a yummy cake for Mellow Yellow's birthday party, but it has been stolen!

A clue is found involving various color mixtures, teaching children about color combinations.

Can Detective Stan find the culprit and save the party before it is too late?

Feelings on the Farm

Farmer Cody's animals are having a lot of different feelings today. Cranky or silly, happy or sad, it is important to understand emotions and how they make you feel.

A playful social emotional learning book that supports healthy emotional intelligence.